You Know It!
SAMMY
the Steiger
Gotcha!
FRANKIE
the Farmall
CODY
the Combine
Hey Dudes!
BAILEY
the Baler
Go Team!
KELLIE
the Combine
Awesome!
PETER
the Patriot Sprayer
VROOM!
SCOOTER
the Case IH Scout
Let's Do It!
TAMMI
the Tiller
Details!
EVAN
the Early Riser Planter

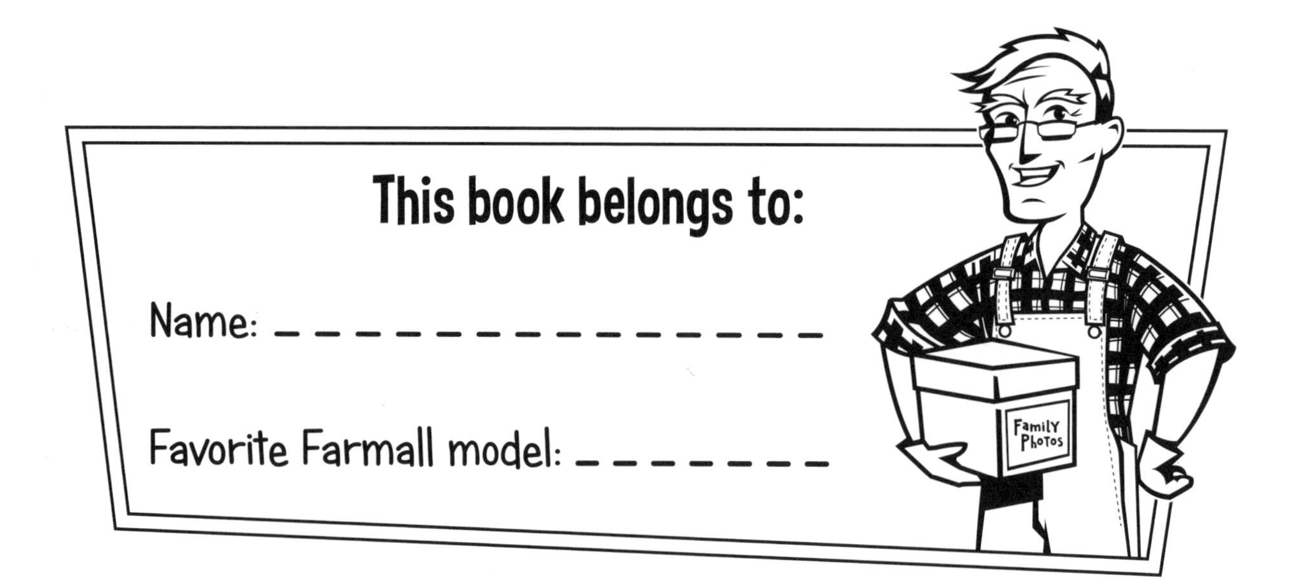
This book belongs to:
Name: _ _ _ _ _ _ _ _ _ _ _ _ _ _ _ _ _ _
Favorite Farmall model: _ _ _ _ _ _ _ _
Family Photos

Farmall in the Family

with Casey & Friends

Let's go on a farm adventure back through time!

Our family has lived on Happy Skies Farm for many generations. We have photos and papers from more than 100 years ago!

Family Photos

1910 | GREAT-GREAT GRANDPA JAMES

Farming in the Early 1900s

When I lived on Happy Skies Farm, we didn't have a tractor to grow crops and do chores. I had a team of horses to power my farm. That's me and my team raking hay into windrows.

Horses take longer to complete a job, so farms were smaller back then.

A large part of the farm was used to feed and care for the animals, too.

1928 | GREAT GRANDPA HENRY

The Family's First Farmall

My family's first tractor was a Farmall Regular. Farmall was the first all-purpose tractor made to work in row crops. It could plow, plant, and cultivate!

Since farmers could do more with one tractor than with a team of horses, farms began to grow.

1930 | GREAT UNCLE JACK

Making the Farmall for Everyone

I helped build Farmall tractors at the Farmall Works plant in Rock Island, Illinois. At its busiest, the Farmall Works plant made 350 tractors a day and employed 5,000 workers.

ARMALL TRA
FARMALL
FARMALL

1932 | GREAT GRANDPA HENRY

Quick-Attachable Machines

My Farmall 12 and its "Quick-Attachable Machines" helped me do many jobs from plowing, mowing, and raking to cultivating and planting.

FARMALL

These tools could be attached or removed in minutes. Today, we call them attachments.

1936 | GREAT UNCLE JOHN

The Great Color Change

Farmall tractors weren't always red. When they were first made, they were painted battleship gray. In 1936, the color changed to Harvester Red No. 50. From that day on, Farmall tractors were painted their famous red color.

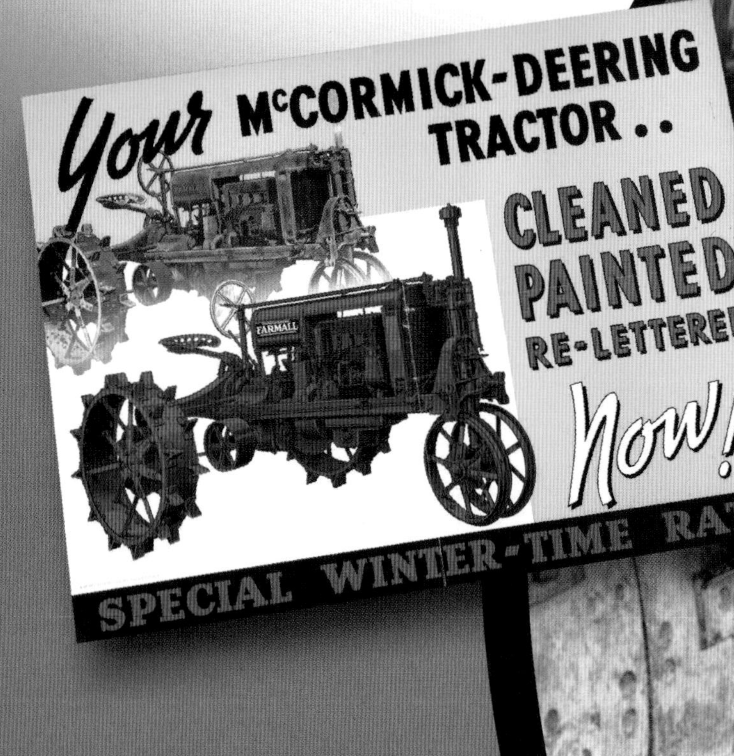

Harvester Red No. 50 is trademarked. That means only Farmall can use that color!

1939 | COUSIN FRANK

Culti-Vision Helps Farmers See More

It's very important for farmers to see where they are driving their tractors. So, we designed Culti-Vision. It moved the tractor driver to the right of the engine so they could see the rows of plants ahead.

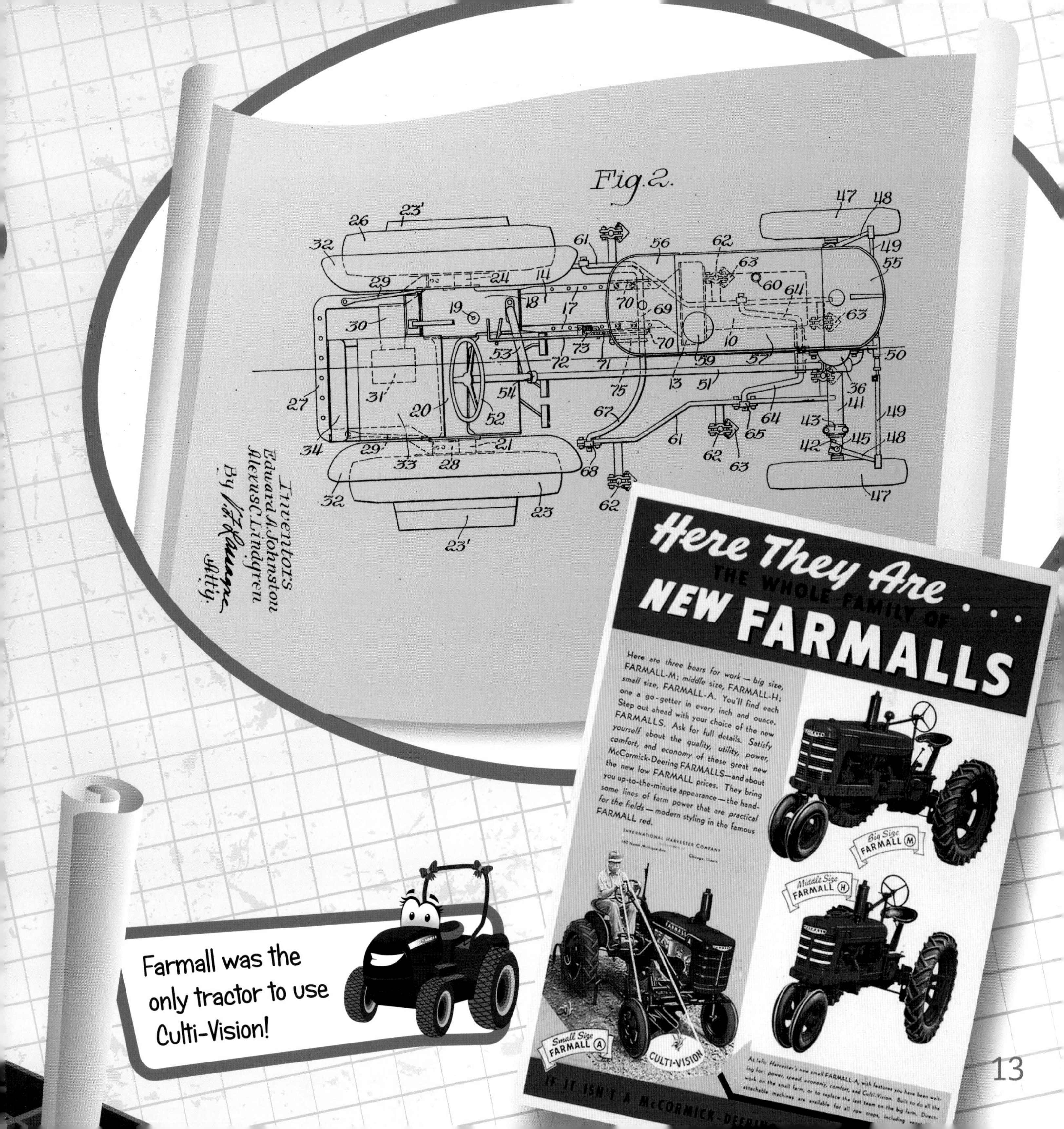

Farmall was the only tractor to use Culti-Vision!

1944 | GREAT GRANDMA IRMA

Tractorettes on the Farm

When we bought our Farmall M, I went to school to learn how to use it and keep it in good working condition.

My friends and I worked hard at growing crops for food. We were called Tractorettes because we had special training to help our communities in times of need.

FARMALL
FARMALL

1947 | GRANDPA BOB

Farmall at the Fair

When I was young, my family would visit the state fair and stop at the International Harvester booth. That's where I saw the new Farmall Cub. This small tractor was designed to replace two or three horses on a farm. Plus, it had 16 quick-change implements to help it do many different jobs.

come! Come on in!

The Cub was one of the most popular Farmall models ever made.

Pull the TA Lever for More Power

Farmall Super M-TA tractors worked faster and with more power than ever before. They could go 10 speeds forward and two in reverse.

It could change speeds instantly when moving over tough spots in the field. Plus, Farmall Super M-TA tractors could travel at slow speeds and still have a lot of power for implements. This was amazing!

FARMALLS
TA means Torque Amplifier-driven.
Mc CORMICK FARMALL
SUPER M-TA TORQUE AMPLIFIER

1956 | GRANDMA BETTY

Electrall Electrifies the Farm

Electricity on the farm wasn't always reliable. That was a problem when it came to farm chores. We used an Electrall generator attached to our Farmall 400 for reliable, mobile electric power.

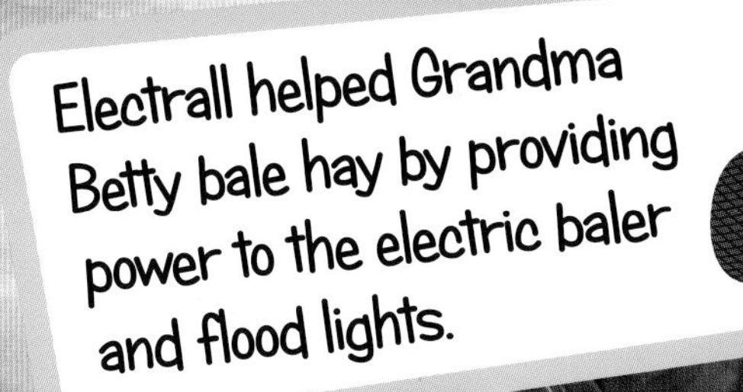

Electrall helped Grandma Betty bale hay by providing power to the electric baler and flood lights.

Now with Hydrostatic All-Speed Drive!

The International Farmall 656 Hydrostatic Drive tractor was a big deal in my day. It allowed the farmer to change speeds while moving. This was useful when working in the fields — the farmer could adjust speeds without stopping.

The Hydrostatic All-Speed Drive was an early form of Continuously Variable Transmission (CVT). CVT is more advanced — it allows the farmer to change speeds from barely moving to top speed without shifting or stopping!

1974 | COUSIN JENNY

IH Makes Tractor History Again!

On February 1, 1974, International Harvester made it's 5 millionth tractor. No other tractor company had made that many tractors before. Can you guess what kind of tractor it was?

It was a Farmall 1066. There was a big party to celebrate!

2003 | UNCLE ZACH

Farmall Tractors are Reborn

International Harvester stopped making Farmall tractors when I was a kid. But when I was old enough to have my own farm, Farmall made a comeback.

They were the right size for doing chores around the farmyard.

A Big History of Tough Little Tractors

I rely on Farmall tractors to help me farm all — just like my family before me. This farm adventure continues with me!

FARMALL

GLOSSARY

ALL-PURPOSE

having many uses

ATTACHMENT

a tool that goes on a tractor and is used for special jobs

CONTINUOUSLY VARIABLE TRANSMISSION (CVT)

allows vehicles to change speeds without the help of the driver

CROP

a plant that farmers grow

CULTIVATE

to prepare soil to make it healthy for growing plants

CULTI-VISION

allowed the driver to see directly in front of the tractor

GENERATOR

a machine that turns energy into electricity

TECHNOLOGY

equipment created by science to solve a problem

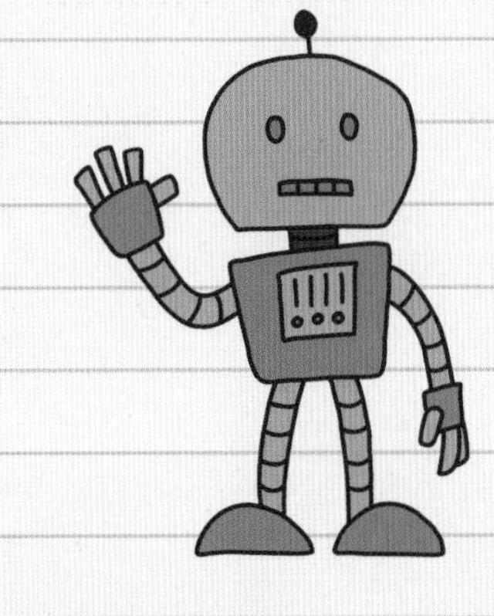

TRADEMARK

a symbol, word, or identity that represents a company or product

WINDROW

hay that is cut and raked into rows

TRACTORETTES

women who were trained to use and maintain tractors in the 1940s

IMPLEMENT

a machine or tool used for a particular task

FUN FACTS!

Over 90 years ago, IH engineers built an experimental Farmall tractor that drove by itself using an electric "remote control" — no farmer in the seat!

Did you know that Farmall square dancing is real? Eight tractors "dance" together for special performances!

Farmall tractors have made many appearances in popular movies, such as *A Christmas Story*!

The first Farmall tractors had steel wheels. It wasn't until the 1930s that tractor companies offered machines with rubber tires.

Many Farmall tractors have been customized for lots of interesting tasks. This tractor was modified to deliver the mail!

The Farmall name originated because the tractor was supposed to do it all — hence the farm-all!

The Farmall Cub tractor was "a cub in size but a bear for work"!

Octane Press, Edition 1.0, September 2023

Library of Congress Cataloging-in-Publication Data

ISBN: 978-1-64234-138-6

1. Juvenile Nonfiction—Transportation—General.

2. Juvenile Nonfiction—Lifestyles—Farm and Ranch Life.

3. Juvenile Nonfiction—Lifestyles—Country Life.

4. Juvenile Nonfiction—Concepts—Seasons

Library of Congress Control Number: 2022944116

Additional photography with permission from the Wisconsin Historical Society p. 2-3 (ID16004),
p. 4-5 (ID12061, ID46101), p. 10-11 (ID49206), p. 12-13 (ID4284), p. 14-15 (ID7244, ID50932, ID50956, ID50955),
p. 17 (ID24564), p. 20-21 (ID24576), p. 31 (ID24576, ID50932), p. 32 (ID86567)

Museum of Innovation and Science p. 21

octanepress.com

Printed in China

Farming keeps me busy, but I love my life!
CASEY
the Farmer
Casey depends on me for the daily weather report!
TILLUS
the Worm
Easy Peasy!
FERN
the Farmall
Be Ready!
BIG RED
the Magnum

MONSTER TRUCK
SUPERSTARS
T0002512
MORTIMER
William Petty

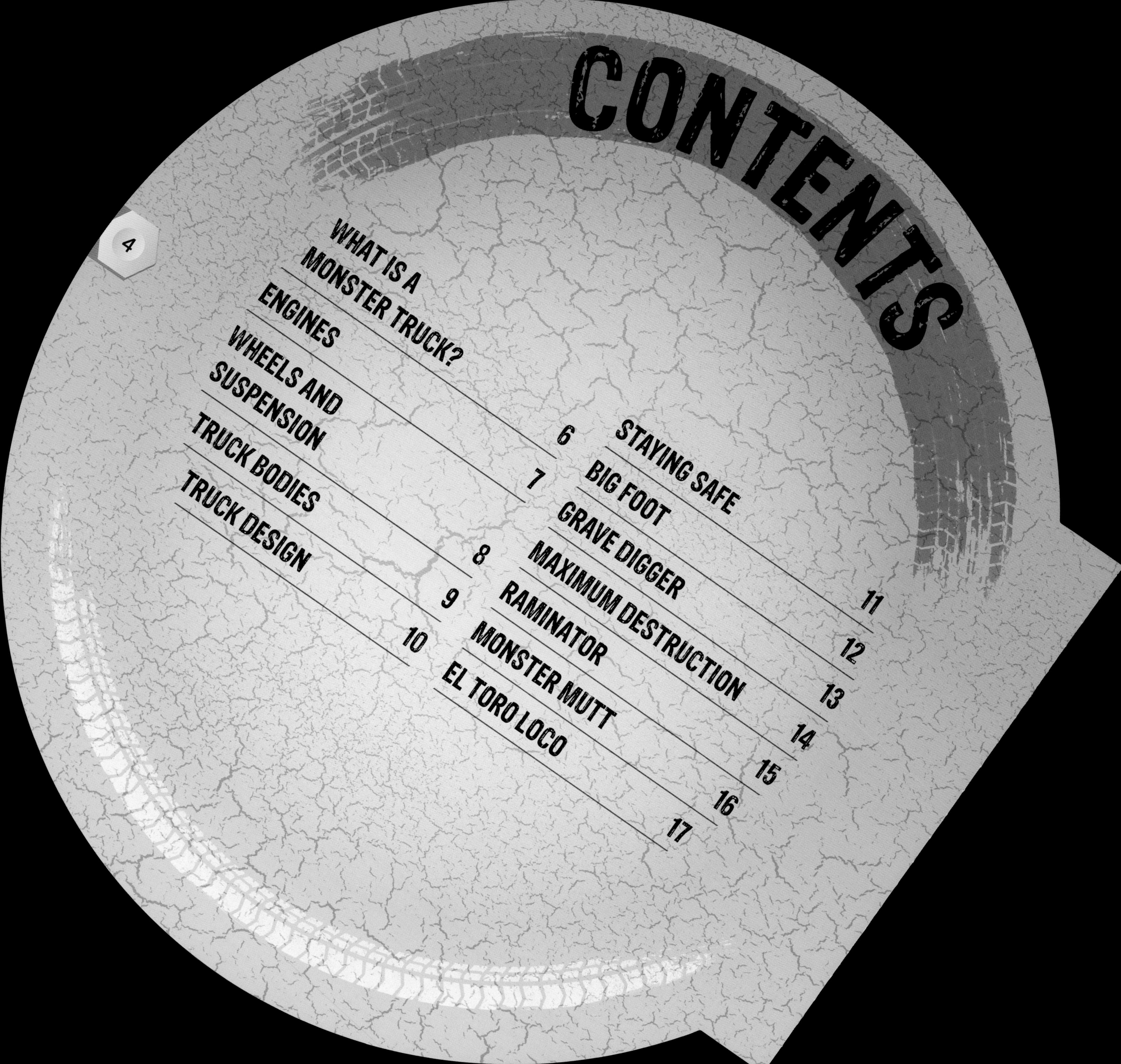

CONTENTS

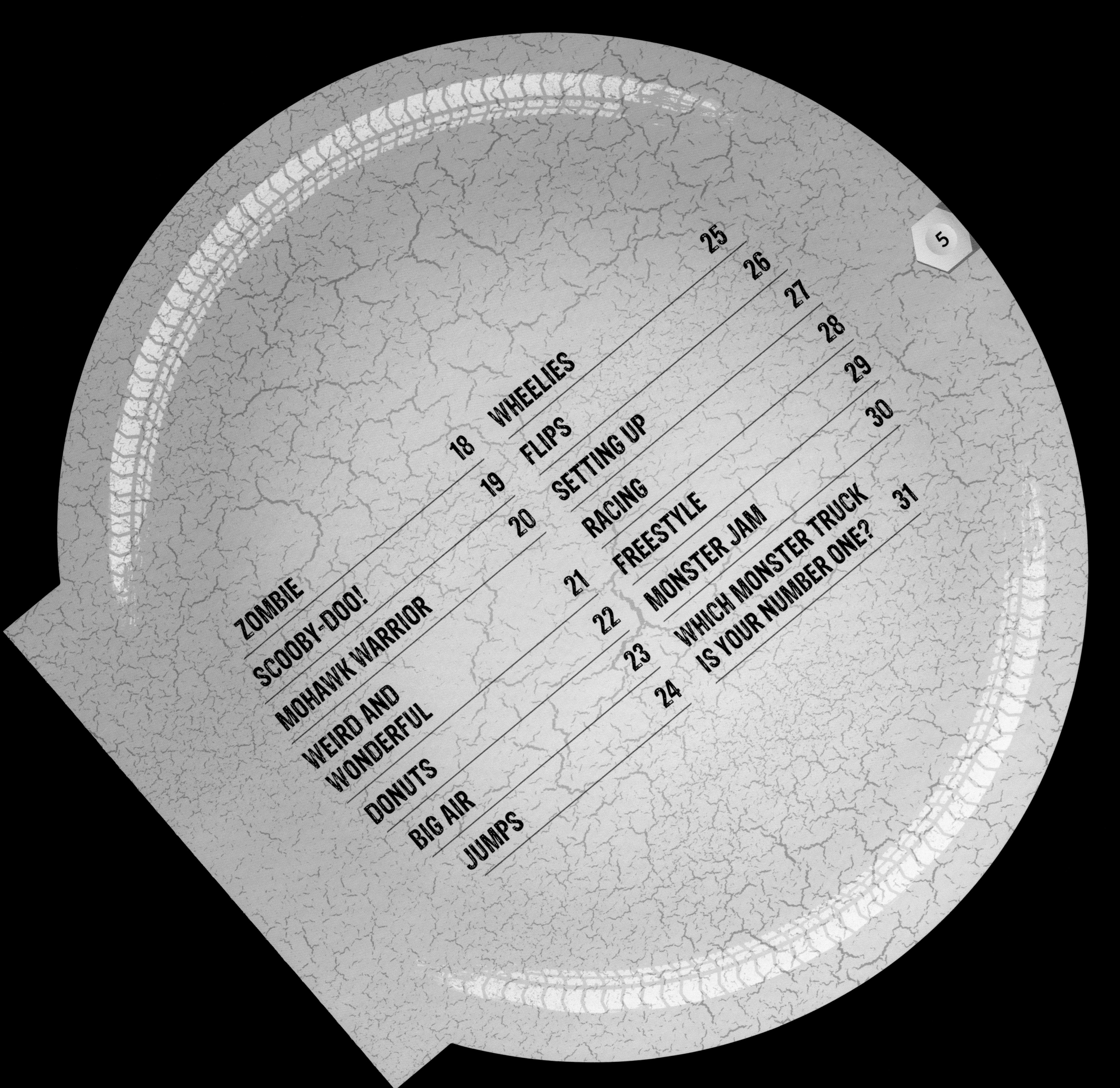

WHAT IS A MONSTER TRUCK?

MIGHTY MONSTERS

When you take a normal-sized truck, and add huge wheels so it towers above the ground, plus a powerful engine and super-strong suspension, you get a monster truck!

THRILL SHOW

Monster trucks take part in noisy, exciting shows, where they race, do incredible stunts, and crush cars beneath their massive wheels. Millions of people go to see monster truck shows each year.

Monster trucks weigh up to 12,000 lbs. (5,440 kg)—more than a white rhino!

ENGINES

ROAAARR!

At the heart of every monster truck is a powerful engine. It makes a deafening roar as it powers the truck around the course, sending it from 0 to 30 mph (48 km/h) in 1.5 seconds!

GAS GUZZLER

Monster trucks run on a fuel called ethanol, and they use a LOT of it. With the amount of fuel a monster truck burns in two minutes, an ordinary car could drive for 90 miles (145 kilometers)!

A supercharged monster truck engine is 5 times more powerful than a pick-up truck engine!

WHEELS AND SUSPENSION

TOWERING TIRES

A monster truck tire can be 5.5 feet (1.68 meters) high—as tall as an adult. They have deep grooves that grip firmly, making it easy to ride over obstacles.

The bar linking the wheels is called an axle, and it has to be very strong.

BOUNCY RIDE

The body of a monster truck is connected to the wheels by incredibly strong springs, called suspension. When the truck hits a bump, or lands off a jump, the suspension lets the truck bounce—not break.

OUTER SHELL

Modern monster trucks aren't made of flat metal like your family car. The outside is a thin shell made of a light material called fiberglass. The shell is made in one piece, like an enormous jello mold!

SAFE INSIDE

Underneath the shell, a monster truck has a strong steel frame called a roll cage. Even if the truck rolls over, the bars of the cage won't bend—keeping the driver safe at all times.

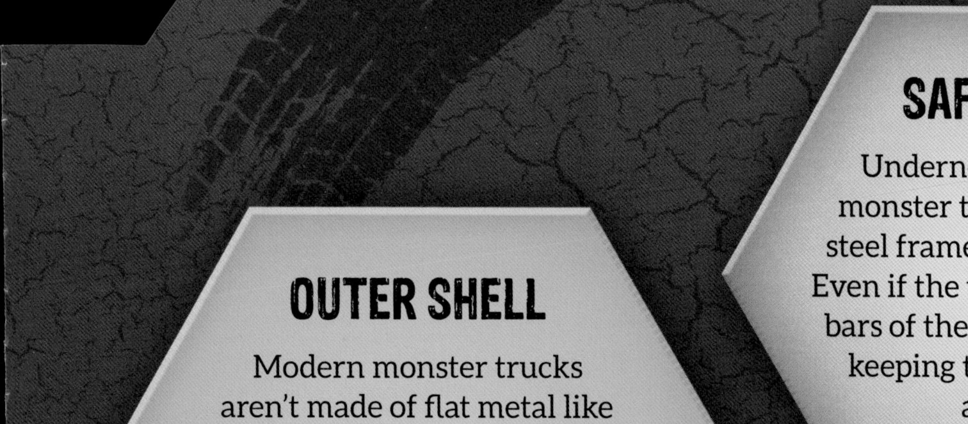

Details like lights and doors aren't real—they're painted on!

TRUCK DESIGN

LOOKING GOOD!

Monster truck teams work hard on cool paint jobs and special features. They don't make the trucks go faster, but fans love how their favorite trucks stand out from the crowd!

HEADS AND TAILS

Some monster trucks have crazy body parts attached to the outside. You might see trucks with sharp teeth, pointy horns, flapping ears, a wagging tail, or even a pair of arms!

Dragon is a monster truck that can breathe fire!

STAYING SAFE

Monster truck wheels are chained to the truck so they can't fly off in a crash.

CRASH!

Monster truck shells get smashed up a lot, but the roll cage protects the driver. Sometimes wheels and axles break too. Then a team of mechanics has to repair them.

SAFETY FIRST

Drivers wear fire-proof suits and helmets in their trucks. Each driver's seat is specially made to fit their body, and their seatbelt straps them firmly to the seat in five places.

BIG FOOT

THE ORIGINAL

In 1976, a man called Bob Chandler invented the first ever monster truck. He added a set of big wheels to his pick-up truck, and started driving it at shows. People loved it!

WORLD RECORD!

BIGGEST TIRES

Bigfoot 5
10 ft. (3.05 m)

Each one of Bigfoot 5's tires weighs 24,00 lbs. (1,090 kg)—as much as a small car!

BIGGER AND BETTER

Bob kept on improving Bigfoot—there have been 20 different versions of Bigfoot over the years. In 1981, Bigfoot was the first monster truck to crush cars by driving over them.

GRAVE DIGGER

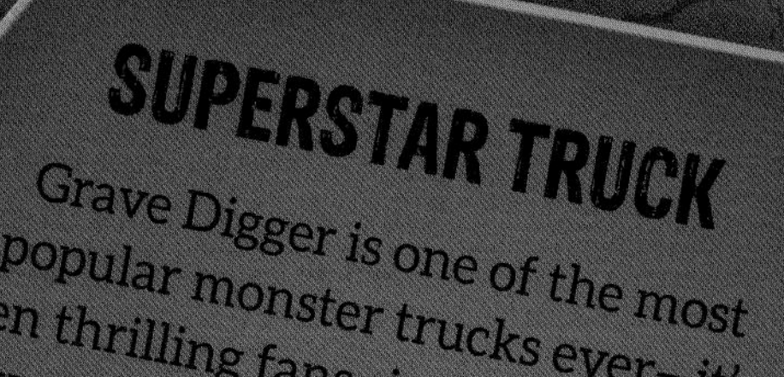

SUPERSTAR TRUCK

Grave Digger is one of the most popular monster trucks ever—it's been thrilling fans since 1982. With its spooky red headlights, this truck is known for driving fast—and crashing a lot!

FAMILY BUSINESS

Grave Digger was created by Dennis Anderson. He drove it in competitions for 35 years. Now his children Ryan, Adam, and Krysten have taken the wheel, carrying on the Grave Digger family tradition.

Each Grave Digger shell is hand painted—it takes 60 hours to complete!

MAXIMUM DESTRUCTION

TO THE MAX!

This spike-covered monster is known as Max-D for short. It's famous for its high-speed rivalry with Grave Digger, and for pushing gravity to the limits with new and exciting tricks.

WORLD RECORD!

MOST DRIVER CHAMPIONSHIPS

Tom Meents
11

In 2015 Max-D got another first: a successful double backflip!

MAJOR TOM

Max-D team leader Tom Meents is one of the most successful monster truck drivers ever—he's an 11-times world champion. He was also the first person to land a monster truck backflip.

RAMINATOR

FINE TUNED

Brothers Tim and Mark Hall knew their truck Raminator was fast. But they wanted to know HOW fast. They improved the engine and gears until they were ready to test it.

Raminator burns fuel 700 times faster than a car!

WORLD RECORD!

FASTEST MONSTER TRUCK

Raminator
99.1 mph
(159 km/h)

SPEED DEMON

In December 2014, Mark Hall drove Raminator at top speed on a Formula 1 track in Texas. He set a new record for the fastest ever monster truck—99.1 mph (159 km/h)!

MONSTER MUTT

TOP DOG

With its trademark ears and a tail that wags as it races round the course, this dog is a fan favorite. In 2010 it showed off its tricks with the top score in the freestyle World Finals.

Monster Mutt's body has evolved over the years—now it's more dog than truck.

A BREED APART

As well as the original Monster Mutt, there is now a dalmatian and a rottweiler version. The driver of Monster Mutt Dalmatian wears spotted overalls to match their truck's paintjob!

EL TORO LOCO

RAGING BULL

This fearsome truck's name means "the crazy bull" in Spanish. As well as the classic red and orange design, El Toro Loco has ridden out in black, yellow, and ice blue versions.

RIDE 'EM, COWGIRL!

El Toro Loco driver Becky McDonough wanted to race monster trucks since she went to a show aged 14. When she's driving, the bull wears a pink bandana on one of its horns.

The driver of El Toro Loco can make steam shoot from its nose!

ZOMBIE

PEOPLE'S CHOICE

This undead monster was the winner of a competition where the public chose which truck they wanted to see made. Its fans show their support by dressing up as zombies!

UNDEAD ARMY

There have been many different versions of this truck over the years, including Skeleton, Female Zombie, and Burned Zombie. The latest is the fearsome Fire Zombie.

Zombie's scary waving arms are its most famous feature.

SCOOBY-DOO!

MYSTERY MACHINE

This high-octane hound is based on everyone's favorite mystery-solving cartoon Great Dane. It's a crazy cross between a pick-up truck and a giant dog!

GREAT DAMES

Girls rule at the all-female Team Scooby-Doo! In 2015, Scooby-Doo! Driver Nicole Johnson became the first woman to land a successful monster truck backflip.

The dangling Scooby-Doo dog tag is this truck's trademark.

MOHAWK WARRIOR

HAIR RAISING

Mohawk Warrior is based on a van, but with a striking addition: a giant spiky "mohawk" hairstyle sticking up from its roof! It was the first truck to do two backflips in a row.

Mohawk Warrior is famous for pulling off perfect wheelies.

WILD STYLE

This monster truck took its name from George Balhan, who was its first driver. He had a wild mohawk hairstyle too—he had to squeeze it into his helmet to drive!

WEIRD AND WONDERFUL

STRANGE SHAPES

Megalodon is a monster truck in the shape of a giant prehistoric shark. Not scary enough for you? How about Higher Education—it's a school bus with monster wheels!

WORLD RECORD!

LONGEST MONSTER TRUCK

Sin City Hustler
32 ft. (9.75 m)

Sin City Hustler is a monster limousine!

RIDING HIGH

Some special monster trucks, called ride trucks, have space to carry passengers. A ride truck called Sin City Hustler is the longest monster truck ever—it's 32 feet (9.75 meters)!

DONUTS

IN A SPIN

For this dizzying trick, drivers spin their trucks round and round on the spot. In donut competitions, they try to spin as long and fast as they can without tipping over.

SPECIAL WHEELS

Monster trucks have four-wheel drive—all four wheels are powered by the engine. They also steer with all four wheels, which helps the driver spin in a really tight circle.

Don't stand too close—pulling a donut sprays dirt everywhere!

BIG AIR

Monster truck tires and suspension cushion the landing.

SAFE LANDINGS

To land safely, a driver has to keep the wheels of their truck spinning fast while it's in the air. If they don't, they could flip over forward when they land.

FLYING MONSTERS

Even though they weigh 5 tons, monster trucks make jumping 30 feet (9 meters) into the air look easy. The secret to catching big air is to hit the ramp doing at least 40 mph (64 km/h).

JUMPS

BIGGER AND BETTER

Drivers are always thinking of new incredible stunts to entertain fans. Sometimes they jump over other monster trucks. In 1999, Bigfoot 14 jumped over a Boeing 727 airliner!

WORLD RECORD!

LONGEST JUMP

Bad Habit
237 ft. 7 in.
(72.42 m)

Bad Habit hit 85 mph (137 km/h) during its record-breaking jump.

ONE GIANT LEAP

The record for the longest jump is held by Joe Sylvester, driving Bad Habit. In 2013 he leapt an incredible 237 feet 7 inches (72.42 meters)—as long as six school buses!

WHEELIES

TWO WHEELS GOOD

A skilful driver can make the front of their truck lift off the ground, and drive along on just the back wheels. It takes good balance, otherwise the truck might fall back onto its roof.

WONDER WHEELIE

When a truck lands a jump, it can do a trick called a slap wheelie. That's where it hits the ground front wheels-first, then bounces onto its back wheels—and stays there!

In a reverse wheelie, a truck drives on its front wheels instead.

FLIPS

SPECTACULAR STUNT

A backflip is when a truck does a backward somersault, and lands on its wheels—or, if it goes wrong, on its roof! It's one of the most exciting tricks.

WORLD FIRST

In 2017, fans saw The Mad Scientist do the world's first-ever monster truck front flip! It did it by pulling a wheelie, then hitting a ramp at high speed, sending it tumbling forward.

WORLD RECORD!

FIRST FRONT FLIP
The Mad Scientist
2017

Speeding up a steep ramp or wall is the key to a backflip.

SETTING UP

BUILDING THE TRACK

Getting a stadium ready for a monster truck show is a huge job. First the ground has to be protected with wood and plastic. Then diggers move in to build obstacles out of earth.

CAR CRUSHING

Crushing cars and vans with their huge wheels is what monster trucks do best. Old vehicles are moved into position with forklift trucks, ready to be squashed!

It can take 7,500 tons of earth to make a monster truck track!

RACING

SPEED DEMONS

Fans love to see monster trucks race—these machines go fast! They have the same engines as dragsters, super-fast cars that race at high speeds down a straight track.

HEAD TO HEAD

In monster truck racing, two trucks compete to see who can finish the course first. Then the winners race against each other, until one truck is crowned the fastest.

Sometimes monster trucks race side-by-side along a straight track.

FREESTYLE

ALL ABOUT STYLE

In a freestyle competition, trucks have two minutes to do as many impressive stunts as they can—without crashing! Drivers study the course and plan their run carefully.

CROWD PLEASING

A team of judges give trucks points out of 10 for their freestyle stunts. The points are added up, and the truck with the most wins. At some shows it's the crowd who vote!

Sometimes trucks compete to do the best wheelie or donut.

MONSTER JAM

BIG SHOW

Monster Jam is the biggest monster truck show around. Every year there are hundreds of Monster Jam shows all around the world, and millions more fans watch on TV.

DOUBLE WINNER

Monster Jam trucks compete to be champions in racing and freestyle. Tom Meents is the only driver to win both competitions in the same year—he's done it twice!

The Monster Jam World Final is the most spectacular show of the year.